Shadows

Of The

Brigade

12 Squared

r.w. hobson

2015© Copyright by r. w. hobson
Shadows of the Brigade
12 Squared

Printed in the U.S.A.

ISBN:**978-0692378632**

Website: Hobbitthouse.com

Publishing Services: DMBookPro.com

SHADOWS OF THE BRIGAGE

12 SQUARED

<u>Storyline:</u>
The story of aging, deep-ops warriors who are assigned to assassinate the President of the United. States.

<u>Background:</u>
Deep-ops warriors had carried out many missions over the years which facilitated government upheaval and overthrow of dangerous, corrupt men and women all over the world. Missions entailed rescue of hostages, military junta training and assassination. All missions were referred to as 'All in a days work'.

These deeply patriotic and secretive men, who had once numbered twelve, were now moving toward what possibly could be their last mission. The <u>12 Squared</u> survivors were but four remaining souls; four men in their early sixties, who with a new team member and a young Arab, would attempt the assassination of the man who just two years earlier had been elected President of The United States.

<u>Characters:</u>

Andy Brouch	aka	Bronk
William Quandt	aka	Party
Sherman Fulman	aka	Sherm
Larry Brantloff	aka	Brandy
Jim Bartell	aka	Butter
Alli-Allesia Mohammad	aka	Allie-Mo

Story line development: JUNE 2009

Chapter 1

The south has always been known for great bars and restaurants, but 'Butter & Dave's Sports Bar and Grill' in Andersonville, Georgia was always at the top of anyone's list for great food and true to their motto, 'The Coldest Beer In The South'.

Butter and Dave did not use refrigeration to get to cold beer. They did it with crushed ice in twelve foot long farm watering troughs. At Butter & Dave's there were ten troughs which provided one hundred and twenty feet of *ice cold beer.* The troughs were mounted on wheels and were divided into sections by movable solid oak panels. Each day before the ice was replenished, the quantities and space allocated for each brand of beer was determined, Once the troughs were full of beer, the ice was heaped upon the bottles and cans. If someone wanted <u>cold</u> beer,

Butter and Dave's Sports Bar and Grill, in Andersonville, Georgia, had it.

Oh, and if anyone came in looking for some European, South American, Mexican or other specialty brew of foreign origin, they quickly found that they were in the wrong bar. American beer was the *only* beer served in Butter & Dave's. It was the American way by their reckoning... brew, buy and drink American beer. Butter and Dave had early on discovered that their customers quickly abandoned their acquired taste for specialty beers in order to eat the fantastic food and drink "The Coldest Beer In The South".

Andy B., the only name locals had really known him by since he stepped out of a black 1975 Cadillac convertible into the hot summer afternoon on July 4, 1999. He was a handsome, well proportioned, sturdy, reserved, middle aged man who seemed to fit in with all the town folk in Andersonville. Andy B. was not one for much small talk and kept a low profile with everyone. The small, well kept bungalow at the end of South Street, near the creek and the city park, was home base for him. He paid cash for the property, did a few repairs and updating on the house and re-landscaped the yard in October of 1999. He seemed to enjoy the home and the quiet surroundings as though they were a form of refuge. He would be away from Andersonville on irregular and sometimes extended periods of time. Andy B. never talked about his travels or personal life. He had become one of the regulars at Butter & Dave's.

Now, thirteen years further into his life, on a late and lazy summer afternoon, the vibration of his cell phone in his shirt pocket, both surprised and annoyed him. Whoever was calling was interrupting his time with his cold beer at Butter & Dave's. He looked at his phone and without hesitation took a small black address book from his shirt pocket and retrieved a ballpoint pen from his cap.

"Andersonville... Go," he said into the phone.

He wrote down a series of numbers and letters of the alphabet on the small pages of his book.

"Copy... Confirm."

With that, he returned the cell phone and the black book to his shirt pocket and the pen into the hole in back of his ball cap. Now, back to the beer.

CHAPTER 2

The nation had just gone through an election eighteen months earlier which had yielded one of the most historic and unusual results in the great history of The United States. Liberals and the so-called disenfranchised American voters had succeeded in electing a, at least partially black man to be the President of The United States. While the "we hope for the best" and the "we believe in change for the country" affiliates were absolutely moon struck by this charismatic young politician, there were grave concerns being voiced by the various factions who foresaw the possibly bad things which might be in store for America. This concern was especially true within the ranks of those who served, returned and suffered through the years following Viet Nam. There was an adamant distrust of this anti-military, community organizer who was so critical of the United States military position in the world. It was more than distrust which existed within the brigades which had gone before and lived their duty to country. The old soldiers smelled a rat and the movement to do something about the smell was fast taking form.

Even though their bodies were older and their hair was either gray or even gone, the shadows of these patriots were clearly visible as they were cast over their love of country and dedication to The Constitution of The United States of America.

The disgust with the highest echelons of the current military establishment, which had evolved since Viet Nam and had further been fostered by *fair war* policies and practices in the mid east campaigns, was at an all time high among the members of the brigades which had preceded them. The years had created a hard crust on a few super patriots who were now entering the last part of their lives. These few had become determined in their resolve to not let the America they had grown up in disappear into a socialist quagmire, to be run by political elitist. Something had to be done for the future generations. There was a defined call to action.

Chapter 3

Andy drank his beer and paid his tab. As he stepped into the late afternoon sunshine his eyes, even shaded by the dark tint military sun glasses, struggled to adjust to the brightness. He walked west on Main Street toward the setting sun. How appropriate that the remainder of his life was also moving into a setting sun, especially as this current mission was developing for him and his brother of arms.

The serene, peaceful nature of Main Street and the seven streets which intersected before he got to South Street would be a far cry from what he could expect within the coming weeks. He was now given to contemplate if and when would be the last time he would unlock his front door. He slid the key into the lock and turned it easily to the right.

After grabbing a quick look at his e-mail, he took the small black book from his shirt pocket, turned to his last insertion and compared each number and letter to a scatter chart of the alphabet on the printout he had received just two days ago. Each number and letter from the black book denoted a particular letter on the scatter chart. CHICAGO. What ever was about to happen on the next mission would take place in Chicago. At least it was not some swampy-assed jungle in some god-forsaken country on the other side of the world. A schedule would arrive within the next forty eight hours per the instructions from those on high.

CHAPTER 4

He had been through so many military and now civilian operations that the one thing he had learned to do was sleep when he had the chance. He had lived by the idea of *plan for what your enemy can do, not what you think he might do.*

His sleep had seemed strangely uneasy. It was 4:00 AM and he was awake.

"Never let *what-ifs* get between your ears," he told himself out loud as the coffee maker worked its magic. Still, he was slightly annoyed and mused that it must be his sixty-one years influencing him. His workout routine was more rigorous than normal. There seemed to be a drive to push for just a little more with each of his daily exercises.

Once the grass was mowed and his flowers watered and fertilized, Andy made a sandwich for lunch and sat down in the front porch swing to replenish his energy with the chicken sandwich and the tall mug of sweet tea. As he rocked slowly, he noted to himself that front porch swings were a missing element in the modern day life for most people. That thought process had figured into his recent thoughts of complete retirement.

By assuming such a non-descript and non-attention-getting persona in the small town of Andersonville, he did not really expect anyone to determine where or who he was. The alarm system and surveillance network he had installed for his house gave him a feeling that he had not experienced on any of his missions. He had learned never to feel too secure, but once inside his house, he felt safe. He kept hashing over the thought of retirement.

After lunch he puttered around in the four stall garage he had built as part of the renovation on the house. He wiped down the new black Tahoe which he had purchased from a guy who owned a GMC dealership in Virginia. The Tahoe was sold as a dealer demonstrator vehicle. Due to the special relationship he had with Larry (Brandy) Brantloff, there was only one hundred and forty miles on the odometer when Andy took possession. The dealer was willing and all to happy to sell the Tahoe to a friend of Brandy's at such a reasonable price.

"Know what the square of 12 is?" William (Party) Quandt had once asked just before the shooting started in a dingy, smelly warehouse in Panama some twenty years ago.

"144," whispered Brandy, the numbers guy in the group.

"Right," whispered Party. I want us to remember that the twelve of us on this night are squared up and represent 144 of any force on the face of this planet."

He took one more look over the retaining wall which separated them from the twenty some odd armed men who were protecting the stacks of illegal, ready-to-ship drugs in the middle of the large bay.

Party winked at his brothers and yelled, "FIRE!!"

CHAPTER 5

The pleasant afternoon temperature and low humidity made the walk to Butter & Dave's seem somehow more enjoyable than Andy could remember over the past five months he had gotten to be at home in Andersonville.

As usual, the bar and restaurant was bubbling with regulars and those in transit or visiting this quaint little piece of heaven in middle Georgia. What a business, he told himself as he made his way to the bar.

Butter was normally bouncing around the restaurant like a high velocity rubber ball, greeting the customers and keeping the staff at peak performance. For right now, he was behind the bar and made note of Andy as he assumed the position on the unoccupied bar stool at the end of the long, polished walnut slab. Butter placed a cold beer on the bar with his left hand and vigorously shook Andy's hand.

"Good to see you Andy B.," Butter said over the noise of the fray.

"Thanks for coming in. Let me know what you need. It's on the house tonight." Butter smiled as he locked onto Andy's stare of surprise. Andy held Butter's eyes as he took his first long drink of beer. Butter broke the eye contact and moved on to his duties. Something was strange.

Andy ordered the sirloin burger with sweet potato fries and his third beer about 7:45 PM. Butter and Dave's was running full tilt. Butter brought Andy's food to him and asked Andy to hang out until about 9:00 PM if he could. Things would slow down by then and that he wanted to discuss something.

"Enjoy the burger... remember it's on the house."

Chapter 6

No one knew much about Butter. He just showed up in town one day in September 2002 in a new Silverado pickup. In his late forties, friendly, well mannered, cautious in speech and genuinely interested in the people he met. He told everyone that he would be in and out of town for the next couple of years, to finish up a couple of jobs he had going, but that he would be making Andersonville his new home town.

When he was in Andersonville, he visited all of the bars and restaurants and had a keen interest in *retiring* to the bar and grill business, but only as an owner and not just another eater and drinker. Everybody commented that he was too young to retire and told him that with a name like Butter, he should open a bakery or breakfast café. He was just a footnote to the town folk until he returned *for good* to Andersonville in February 2004.

Butter terminated his rental agreement on the small house he had occupied for two years and bought a home just a few blocks from the middle of town. He started looking at all of the commercial business buildings that were or could be for sale. He appeared to be more than ready to settle down in Andersonville. He finally settled on the old Woolworth's building, spent six months remodeling the shell that had been mostly forgotten, except by a guy who used it as a distribution and storage facility for his trucking company for two years. Otherwise, the building had just sat quietly on the corner of Broadway and Spring Street, empty and even though a well built structure, had been giving way to time.

The fanfare and novelty of great food, friendly service and 'The Coldest Beer In

Chapter 6

The South', from iced down farm watering troughs, was an instant success. Words of praise spread rapidly and people came from literally everywhere to be a part of the experience. Six years later, life was good for Jim (Butter) Bartell. He would sometime be gone on short vacations, but he always came back to his business in Andersonville.

CHAPTER 7

Business had been good this day, for a Thursday, but had slowed enough for Butter to grab a couple of beers and make his way to the far side of the restaurant and a secluded booth. He had motioned for Andy to join him. Andy wondered what Butter wanted to talk about as he crossed the big dining room and slid into the booth opposite Butter.

Butter offered a toast with his raised beer bottle.

"Here's to the future," he said, while holding Andy's questioning gaze.

"This is a safe place for us to talk," Butter said, "and I will come right to the point of this conversation."

"We have some mutual acquaintances which I have just been made aware of in the last two weeks. This will come as a surprise to you, but I know Party, Sherm, Brandy... and now I know you, Bronk."

Andy's grip on the beer bottle tightened and his eyes left Butter's as he quickly surveyed the room. Once his stare returned to Butter, he said, "What?"

"Same service .... Same master, " Butter said.

"CIA, Black Bird, covert ops," Butter said without moving his eyes.

"I'm a younger version of you, Bronk, and we became who we are and in some ways what we are today, by serving our country outside the rules and parameters of what the signatory government shows on its face everyday. Even though there are a few years between us, we are the same person, and what are the odds that we would settle in the same town?"

Chapter 7

"There's something which makes me wonder about that," Butter said as he relaxed in his side of the booth.

"There's something which bothers the shit out of me as to what you just said... What the hell are you talking about and who the fuck are these people and their Black Bird you mentioned?" Andy asked as he locked hard on to Butter's eyes.

"Exactly the way I would have reacted." Butter said, "And I know I will have to earn your trust. But, our country is under attack and the *powers* are calling a few of the *old dogs* to take care of the situation."

Butter again leaned forward. His voice was deeper and extremely serious.

"Here is the short and sweet. This sorry assed, liberal President is leading a charge to destroy our country and he is to be *remedied from his task.* You are to be part of the remedy if you so choose. I'm just the *fly-over* here tonight. You have to contact Party to verify me and what I have said."

Butter again relaxed against the padded cushion back rest.

"I don't really know you or what you went through in your service, but I'm pleased to know you now Andy and I know that I have surprised you with names and memories of your years gone by. I am you and hopefully we are on the same path of righting the wrong in this great country of ours."

Andy stared into Butter's pale blue eyes for several moments, then abruptly slid to his right and out of the booth. He strode across the dining area and exited the bar into the warm night air.

CHAPTER 8

His walk home was filled with thoughts of Party, Sherm, Brandy and his other band of brothers during Viet Nam and the later years when he served on missions with the Black Bird. Some of the guys were dead now. All of the remaining were older men today, but all had served their country in black ops missions all over the world. Their fight for freedom and liberty for the citizens of the United States seemed never to be over. The only things that would really end their mission were time and death.

The group, of Andy's time, was succumbing to one or both. He had already felt the presence of the passage of time, but he wasn't ready for the death part. Andy may not have been on missions during the past several months, but his acceptance of the new and younger generation of super secret ops men and women seemed to be the natural turn of events. It was a time thing.

He decided during his walk home that he would wait until morning to contact Party. He knew that by now, Butter had already reported that the fly-over was completed. It would be up to Party to determine the success of the ten thousand foot visual approach. He wondered why Party had chosen to have Butter introduce himself in this way.

Chapter 9

Andy experienced a restless sleep pattern, but was surprisingly refreshed when he awoke at 4:30 AM. Coffee was the first priority of the day. With a big mug of steaming black coffee in front of him on his desk, he removed the ream of plain copy paper from the middle desk drawer and then carefully lifted the false bottom of the drawer. He palmed the small, black sophisticated phone and prepared to call Party. The first thing he wanted to know was *who in hell was Jim 'Butter' Bartell.* The second question would be why hadn't Party contacted him prior to last night to tell him about the situation.

After punching in a series of numbers which he had used fewer than five times since the new phone had arrived three years ago, he heard the familiar clicks which seemed old fashioned, given all the elaborate technology, but he knew that each click took his call deeper into a communication realm to which only a select few people had access.

"Bronk."

"Hello, Party ... Been a while"

"Busy in the Mideast. That fucking group of sand crawlers is something else. We should have turned the whole god-damned place into hot sand back in the 70's. None of them are worth a flying fuck, but the pay is good and the adventure never ending." Party paused in his characteristic rapid fire dissertation.

"How are you, Bronk?"

"I was calm on the pond until last night. I feel a little blind sided to tell you straight out. The fly-over was interesting and effective, but why in the hell did you elect to do it this way, and who the shit is this Butter?"

"He's the new generation, Bronk. We're being replaced at a rapid clip, you understand. Good man. He's one of us and was one of the best at the trade while on competitive government service. Wanted to back off and give *his* replacements a chance on the stick. Kinda burned out, I guess. He wanted to give civilian life a try for a while, but the political situation has gotten out of hand and we can count on him for this mission."

"How 'bout you, Bronk? Have you got one more gallon in the tank for this thing? I know that you don't have a lot of information, but it will not be much of anything new for the act itself. It's the political fallout in the streets of the ghettos that will be a possible management crisis. But, as always, there seems to be a plan and series of events which hopefully will deflect scrutiny and the blame off the establishment.

"I'm thinking about a cabin on the lake myself after this mission. I find I get tired out more easily now that 65 has come and gone. I've lived the adventure and now I'm thinking about living life. So, do you want to *be* one more time, Bronk?"

"Let's meet and talk. I need some details and will decide if my ass has the push for the mission. The plane?"

There was a brief pause, and Andy prepared to write.

"AQ439YZBAK... later my friend."

Andy pulled the sheet of paper which contained the letter and number matrix out of his desk. The plane would pick him up at Chamblee, DeKalb-Peachtree executive terminal, the following week on Wednesday, at 10:30 PM.

CHAPTER 10

The Citation's engines had barely shut down when the cabin hatch opened and the steps descended to the tarmac. Andy hastily covered the forty yards between the terminal and the plane. Once he and his small leather travel bag were inside the fuselage, the steps retracted, the door closed and the engines sprang to life.

Choosing the right front seat just behind the bulkhead, Andy settled in. It crossed his mind that this could possibly be his next to last flight on the Citation. His last flight he hoped would be back to Georgia and home to Andersonville. What a life, he mused to himself, as he gazed around the sparse yet luxurious cabin which had been re-furbished since he was last on the plane. Party kept his guys comfortable before there was a chance for things to become very uncomfortable.

"Shit, how did you get to here, man?" Andy said out loud. "How did you get to here?"

Chapter 11

Andy was lost deep within his thoughts about his life and black ops mission in which he had participated over the years when the Citation's engines were slowed and a wide right banking turn was made in a final approach to Andrews Air Force Base. He thought many times of how ironic the scenario that a black ops organization, run by a civilian, was able to operate out of Andrews. It was a case where the best cover was right out in the open. It was 1:22 AM.

Party's status and reputation of taking on and successfully completing missions the US military and other ops groups could not touch was legendary among those with a need to know. He and his people had been the *go to* factor for some of the most secret and sensitive situations in the world. Due to experience, proper planning and execution of the plan, Party and his band of brothers had a one hundred percent success story in results.

The non-descript one story hanger was located near the southeast corner of Andrews. Although it appeared to be possibly a storage facility, once inside that perception immediately was modified. It was exemplary in cleanliness and presentation of a high tech jet equipment and operational center.

The Citation had cut its lights as it cleared the active zone and rolled slowly toward a large blacked-out rectangle in the side of the building. Engine whine was almost negligible as the plane coasted to a stop some one hundred feet from the open hanger door. There was not a single light to be seen in the entire facility. Within a few seconds, Andy felt the jet moving again and he knew that the mule was towing the Citation inside the windowless hanger.

Chapter 11

There was total darkness as the exit door of the jet opened and the stair extended. Andy sat quietly until he heard the vacuum hiss the large hanger door indicating that the building was again completely sealed. He then grabbed his travel bag from the leather seat opposite him and ducked through the fuselage door and down the steps.

The hanger was totally void of light except for the one-half inch wide, cloudy green line embedded in the floor. The emitted light was almost indiscernible and extended into the pitch blackness of the surroundings. Andy stepped briskly along the green light as he had done so many times before.

When he reached the small green circle of light, he stopped and placed his hand on a pedestal to his right. A lock clicked, and the unseen door in front of him opened. Andy stepped past the threshold three paces and held position. The door closed behind him and the direct lighting began a soft transition from darkness to visible illumination. After the total darkness, his eyes adjusted to once again receiving light waves. Accustomed to the light, he proceeded down the wide hall to the thick bullet proof glass door which opened as he approached.

When Andy entered the *war room* with its large illuminated wall maps of the world, wooden situation table and a computer banked briefing area, he saw his old friend and warrior brother, Party, sitting in one of the large leather briefing chairs, smoking a cigar and studying a Jack Daniels on the table in front of him.

Party literally popped from the chair, gave a snappy salute to his fellow patriot and then held out his hand for one of Andy's resoundingly firm handshake.

Chapter 11

"God, you're looking good, Bronk! Civilian life has been treating you well over these last several months."

He threw his left arm around Andy's shoulders and exerted an almost crushing hug to his comrade.

"You know, that hugging bullshit may have not been the thing to do back in the day, but what the shit... everybody does it today." Party laughed his gruff and non-pretentious laugh.

"I know you have been sitting a while so I won't ask you to sit down if you need to stretch out. How 'bout a Jack to get the flow started?"

"You bet," Andy replied.

"You may say to the contrary, Party, but if we both look this fucking old, maybe we need to re-evaluate our program. Where has our youth and time gone?"

Andy raised his glass and toasted, "Here's to Jack and us."

"Hell, Bronk, I don't feel too different than what I remember in the 70's, and I can still do most of the *things* I did, I just don't seem to be able to do them as often."

Party's engaging smile completely obliterated the true man under the mop of white hair and behind the crystal blue eyes. Over the years, Party had been capable of most anything in order to accomplish the mission. Subversion, torture, shoot-to-wound, shoot-to-kill, government overthrow, bribery.... If it was needed to accomplish a result, Party had done it.

"Damn, my friend, it really is good to see you again. I'm glad you came here tonight."

Chapter 11

Party started to sit down in his chair, but before his ass hit the seat, he was back up and gesturing toward the illuminated maps.

"Same god-damned amount of real estate except for Hawaii... its grown a bit since '86, but still the same fucking problems we have always faced. Nothing seems to change over the years except the faces on the bad guys. We deal with one guy or group and another pops up in the same damn place. I still say the biggest mistake the world has made was not dealing with these fucking radical Muslims back in the 70's. We should have brought that shit to an end, because look at what we have now." Party snorted and took a deep drag on his cigar.

"Yep, just look at what we have now.... a Muslim sympathizer in the White House who runs around the on the American taxpayer's dollar, apologizing to the world because he thinks the United States is primarily responsible for the global problems. Well, we have to fix that shit and soon."

"I know you understand that you are preaching to the choir here." Andy said, "But every solution needs a plan. So, what is the plan?"

"Before we go there, I have some explaining to do. You know that I trust and love you as much as any man I have ever worked with. You have been everything a comrade and brother in arm could possibly be. I want to justify my approach to you with Butter. Butter is the real deal. He is an exceptional person and patriot and has for his young age, compared to us, shown that he knows what and how to accomplish the mission.

He will serve as a facilitator with us this time, maybe not in direct personal contact with you, but he will be around and critical to the mission. This plan will take some time and coordination to come to fruition, so feel at ease with Butter. I found it almost remarkable that you two wound up in the same town in Georgia. What are the odds?"

CHAPTER 12

Some twenty year ago, questions and concerns about one of the team had surfaced due to some erroneous information which had almost gotten Andy, Sherm, Brandy and Party killed. That experience haunted the entire organization and a team member, code name Fong, just disappeared. Andy had asked Party, while they were on a mission in Nicaragua, about the situation and was given a.... *Don't ever ask anything about that again,* look. It had always bothered Andy, wondering if Party had taken out one of his own. Quite truthfully, something akin to that was the first thing which had popped into his mind when Butter had surprised him at the restaurant. He immediately realized that if something like that was to be done to any one of the members of the 12 Squared, they would never have seen it coming. There would not have been an introduction of any kind.

"Look, it's almost 03:00. Today is going to be a long day. Let's grab a few winks. Your usual quarters are ready and waiting and I'm tired too. Sherm and Brandy will be here by 09:00 and we can discuss the entire plan with all of us in the room. OK, with you?"

"Sure," Andy said. "My body is telling me that I could use some sleep."

Andy grabbed his travel bag and walked with Party down the wide corridor which led to the well appointed sleeping apartments. He always stayed in the third apartment. There were six apartments in all and four would be occupied for the next couple of days while plans were made for another mission. The magnitude of this mission, on the soil of the United States, could possibly be the most important of their

Chapter 12

long career. The stakes were high and the meaning of *living on the edge of life*, had never been and would never be as great as that which they were about to experience on this mission.

There was tightness in Andy's stomach as he bid Party good night. He really couldn't come to grips with why he had the sensation, and laid it off to the late hour of the night and his thoughts of Fong.

He reached into his travel bag and extracted an especially designed hard rubber door chuck which he placed under the door. He had never used the chock here, only in foreign and unfamiliar settings. It bothered the hell out of him that he was using it tonight, but he was and that was that.

CHAPTER 13

Sleep came with some effort, but the light knock on his door some hours later, woke him easily and he felt refreshed and very much alive.

"Breakfast in about twenty big guy," came Party's voice from the hallway.

"I'm going to crank up some music in the situation room, so be ready to enjoy on your way to chow." Party's voice trailed off as he moved down the corridor.

The jets of the shower were stinging yet soothing to his skin and Andy suddenly felt alive and ready to face the day. He shaved and put on clean clothes. After picking up the door chock and putting it back in his travel bag, Andy almost ran toward the high tech kitchen just off the hanger bay. The music, as advertised, was rocking.

As he approached the large plate glass windows which separated the eating area from the hanger bay, he could see Sherm and Brandy seated at the large round table in the middle of the dining room. Party was just sitting down with a pot of coffee in his hand.

"Can one more aging gentleman join the group?" Andy said as he pushed open the glass door and strode quickly toward his old friends and comrades in all that was patriotic.

"Hey, Bronk, how are you man?" Sherm and Brandy responded almost in unison.

After handshakes, smiles and some cutting remarks about how each other looked, coffee and breakfast were served and past adventures were rehashed... abbreviated versions, but none the less rehashed. Their shared adventures and missions were all they could talk about, because private lives were just that, private.

Chapter 13

None of them really knew about marriage, children, grandchildren or everyday life of the confidants who shared many experiences which could have meant death to any one or all of them. They had become the four survivors of the original twelve men of honor, the Twelve Squared. Death or a decision to not participate anymore had eliminated eight of his brothers. Andy knew that it had happened as part of inescapable human frailty or just growing older and wanting to *go fishing*.

What sat around this table at this moment was all that was left of a group of men who realized their patriotic mission and had been willing to lay down their lives for each mission they had undertaken. They were now aged warriors with precious little time left in their journey.

CHAPTER 14

"Not since Kennedy, has anything like this been attempted," Party slowly announced.

"Reagan didn't count, because that was just some deranged wing nut wanting to get attention. Our mission, gentlemen, is to be a well planned and successful assassination of a President of the United States of America." Party submitted as he surveyed the faces before him.

"It is a very evident truth to the financial magnets, the political elites and the patriots of this great country that this guy has to go," he added.

"Nothing but bad is happening to our country and it is time to turn the ship around and we have been tapped to accomplish that task."

"There will be no sadness in the ranks of the powers which run Wall Street, the politicians in Washington D.C., most of the state houses or even the hard working everyday people who comprise the majority in this great country. No, there will be little sadness there. In fact, it will be *bailing* their asses out of what they got themselves into," Party noted philosophically.

"No, the only sadness and rage will be in the masses who have put their faith and trust in this guy and who were looking to get their share of the pie without doing one god damned thing for it, except just exist.

"Gonna be a tough and rude awakening" Party said as he continued to study the three men around a breakfast table in Virginia.

There was not a blink of eyes, a hint of surprise or sign of repulsion from anyone. It would be just like every other mission they had undertaken over the many years they had been together. It was never personal, just a mission to be successfully completed. It was always just a mission.

"Bronk is the only one of us who hasn't worked with Butter, but since Butter has joined our ranks, Bronk, he has proven to be a solid asset that we can count on," Party continued.

"The only contact we will have with Butter will be via mobile radio. He will be our *preventer* in Chicago, and if we are not successful there, we will move on to Albany. Butter is already in Chicago working on the computer and surveillance cameras so that we are not seen and not blindsided by anything which would link any of us to the mission. His side of things will take a lot of time and detail work. Trust me; he is very good at what he does. We have a two week window this go-round, so if you're ready, let's get down to details."

"Regular assignments, Sherm, commun-ications and recon evaluations, Brady ground facilities, Butter will guide us with visuals, Bronk and I will handle the trigger, and that is where this mission is different from anything else we have ever done. None of us will be the trigger... We have a sixth member to contend with this time."

"We have," Party said with defined words, "A Muslim who will get the shots at an up close and personal range."

"He has a real hard on for the President, because he believes that there is a direct line of responsibility for the massacre of his family in Afghanistan, to the President and a couple of important Saudi Arabia *muckety-mucks* who live in the United States. He believes that the election of the President was bought and paid for by Arab money. He is willing to die for his cause .... Does that surprise any of you?"

"Evidently his father and brother were high level ministers in the government of Afghanistan and were getting ready to blow the whole god damned government corruption scheme out of the water in return for safe passage for themselves and their family to the U.S. Somehow the Saudi powers got wind of the situation through secret information leaks, passed what they knew to Afghanistan and the entire family was slaughtered, probably not only to shut the father and brother up, but to serve as an example to those who might even contemplate anything against the money sucking thugs from either country. That U.S. dollar is god damned powerful and coveted. Remember what Saddam had stacked in his palace?"

"Our boy's name is Allie Allesisa Mohammad. We will call him *Allie-Mo.*

Now, let's look at the plan. We have to be ready in five days."

CHAPTER 15

Andy hardly noticed the roar of the engines and the subtle forward lurch of the Citation. His attention was consumed by the intense young Arab who sat in the rear facing seat across the isle from him. The jet hurtled down the runway and launched into the warm, late afternoon sky.

Allie-Mo had lost his entire family. Andy knew what it was like to lose the people he had loved in his life. His parents had lived into their eighties and had passed silently from this existence with little left to denote that they were part of a population which had lived through some hard times, a few wars and the ever changing landscape of life in modern America. Their oldest son was killed in a motorcycle accident when he was only forty years old. Andy had the task of getting his parents through the trauma;

made all the more difficult when he was serving in Viet Nam and then the constant being away from them as he served with Black Bird all over the world. His parents had led a good life and had given him the basis for becoming a man and standing on his own two feet. His occupation provided him with a great deal of money. He saved, spent on what he wanted, lived the way he wanted to live and never really desired more than what he had in life. Why amass a lot of 'stuff' when you might not survive to enjoy it later in life. Andy's life was a commodity and could have been ended at any time.

Andy had a wife until she could no longer live with the pressure of him being gone away from home so much. She had told him after the second year of marriage that she would not want to get pregnant, knowing that he might not come back. She never knew why Andy was gone, where he was or when he was coming home. There was always plenty of money and the good things in life. She accepted his explanation of special government service, suspected the possibility of another woman and tried for five years to make her life with and without him. She asked for a divorce when Andy was thirty-three years old. He tried to stay in touch, but lost track of her when she re-married and moved to California. His love for her haunted him for several years. His dedication to his secret life and master ruined his marriage and precluded him from ever having another lasting relationship.

He had a tumultuous fuck and suck three years with Marilee, a woman he had met while training some Air Force Special Ops guys in Phoenix, Arizona. She was the epitome of the common white whore and would do just about anything when it came to sex and having a good time. She readily accepted Andy's zest for life and adventure during their first years together. The on-going training in Phoenix for the Air Force and the time between missions proved to be a man's wet dream of what a free and sexually explicit life could be with a woman who seemed to enjoy the ride and the excitement of being with a man like Andy. He knew that she could be fucking around on him while he was away on a mission, and that began to bother him as he grew to care for her and entertain thoughts of making a permanent life with her. As fate would have it, that was never to be.

Andy planned to surprise Marilee when he came back from the Middle East mission which put the final screws to the Hussein regime in Iraq. The Black Bird set up the itinerary and the combined forces of the United States military executed the "Shock and Awe" which brought another dictatorship down.

Chapter 15

As the Citation turned and headed west, Andy's memory drifted back to a disastrous night which never really left his heart and his soul.

Stan had picked Andy up at the airport. He was in Phoenix for a few days and suggested that he be the 'pick-up' guy for Andy's return. Stan had driven the new BMW to show it off as an example of 'Boys and Their Toys'. Amid some catch up conversation, the two men zipped in and out of traffic on the way to Marilee's house. Stan was a stream of information about the specifications of the new "Beamer' and its prowess.

Andy was lost in thought and anticipating a happy surprise reunion with a night of dinner, drinking and sex. The BMW idled nervously as they waited for the traffic light to change and allow Stan to send his new hot toy hurtling up the mountain toward Marilee's house. As the pedestrian timer counted down... 3...

2... 1, Marilee's Honda Pilot sped through the intersection and headed west.

"I'll be damned! Follow her," Andy said, pointing at the Honda.

The light turned green and Stan pressed the accelerator to the floor and the engine responded with a roar and a gut sucking lurch forward. Staying a surveillance distance from Marilee's car, Stan followed her into the flow of traffic which turned north onto the freeway. After two exits, the Honda headed east on Shea Avenue. Stan transitioned in the traffic lane and remained six vehicles behind her. Andy cautioned Stan to stay a safe distance away from the Honda.

"There is no way she knows this car," Stan said with a little excitement in his voice. "We could be right on her ass and she would never know that you were here. Look at me man.... What's this cloak and dagger shit going to accomplish?"

"Just keep it cool," Andy admonished without removing his eyes from the Honda.

With cautious maneuvering, Stan easily kept her vehicle in sight for about four miles where she turned into a small strip shopping center. In the maze of rows and rows of vehicles, they momentarily lost sight of the Honda. Suddenly, Andy saw Marilee walking briskly along the covered walkway. She entered a restaurant named Industrial Burger, a small burger and fries place on the northeast corner of the center.

Stan found a parking place near the bank building and expertly wheeled the BMW into the space. After putting the car in first gear and turning off the ignition, he turned to a very solemn-faced and curiously quiet Andy.

"What now my friend?"

Andy waited silently for about ten minutes and then exited the car and walked slowly by the front of the restaurant and looked inside. Marilee was seated on a high bar stool. Beside her was a tall slender man dressed in slacks, a short sleeved, button shirt and sandals. Of all the shoe styles in the world, he had to have on sandals. "God-damned sandals," Andy said almost out loud.

The sandals guy appeared to take Marilee's presence for granted as he continued for some time to have a very animated and laugh filled conversation with a big-bellied guy to his right. The conversation seemed to go on forever as Andy stood outside the glass door on the east side of the building. Marilee just sat on her stool, looking down at the table and seemingly enduring the robust comments from both men. She feigned a smile a couple of times but was never a part of the interaction. The two men finally seemed to run out of things to say and the fat man said his good-bye and moved on toward the bar.

The sandal guy turned toward Marilee and said something to her. She shook her head in exaggerated affirmation to him, like a dog's reaction of getting excited about being asked if it wanted to go for a car ride.

"Just like Pavlov's dogs.... The mere mention of the right thing, in the right way and the drooling starts," Andy said out loud.

Marilee quickly gathered her purse and literally bailed off of the bar stool. Andy knew by her reaction, after being basically ignored for an hour, that this wasn't her first time with this guy. Sandal guy knew he was assured of getting laid in a few minutes. The fact virtually exploded in the moment.

Marilee got into her Honda and followed the sandal guy's Tahoe out of the parking lot. Stan and Andy, were right on her bumper. The three-vehicle parade traveled east for about two miles and turned north on 93rd Street and then east into a gated condo complex. The Tahoe waited a few seconds at the gate and then entered with Marilee's Honda close behind. The two vehicles traveled about thirty yards and turned right.

Andy had seen enough, but something made him bolt from the BMW and sprint down the sidewalk which bordered the wall surrounding the complex. The garage door on the second condo in from the street was open. The Tahoe was in the garage and Marilee's Honda was pulled in behind it. Sandal guy got some things out of the back of the Tahoe and motioned Marilee to follow him. Marilee

Chapter 15

walked into the garage and the overhead door closed behind her.

Andy stood frozen somewhere between disbelief and reality. This part of his world was shattered. Every fiber of his being wanted to go to the condo and confront the two of them, but what would be the point? The guy didn't know or care about anything but getting a piece of ass for the night and evidently Marilee didn't have any real feeling about the relationship Andy had envisioned. If she had truly cared about a future with him, she wouldn't be fucking sandal guy tonight.

A final note to the relationship he had with her would be that she was the best example of a common, low class, steel town whore that any woman could be.

He, if he had been honest with himself, had known that all along.

Part of Andy's psyche died that night and the devastation of his emotions dictated that he would never again have a meaningful relationship with another woman. Carnal, yes ... meaningful, never again.

Chapter 16

Andy looked over at Allie-Mo who was staring out the window and appeared calm and distant from his surroundings. Andy knew how to do that; not during any mission he had ever been on, but just after, when he was returning from the mission or at home in a safe, familiar setting. Andy speculated as to what must be going on inside the head of a young Arab who would attempt the assassination of the President of the United States.

Part of the irony of the situation was that Allie-Mo was not signed on to this mission having the interest of American citizens and the United States as his motive for such a monumental deed. His was revenge, pure and simple. Unlike the other men on the plane, who accepted this as just another mission, Allie-Mo wanted to kill for pure hatred. Party, Brandy, Sherm and Andy had always compartmentalized the goal line and not the nefarious reason for their assignment. Never had they made the mission personal.

There was little to no conversation as the Citation progressed toward Chicago Midway. In the extreme and everyday air traffic at Midway, the Citation would be just another statistic for the daily log of activity. Each member of the team knew his assignment and had made the appropriate arrangements in order for the mission to be successful.

Brandy would have three vehicles ready at the terminal curb. He had supplied everyone with altered Illinois driver's license. The insurance papers and registration for the vehicles would be in the glove box. Each vehicle would be rigged with enough explosives to make it a scrap heap when it was no longer needed. A special code number was embedded in the cell phones which Sherm had handed out as they left

Andrews that would be activated for the detonation. It was not that the vehicles themselves would yield much information, but a fingerprint, a hair, saliva or other innocuous item might lead to their identities. Nothing could be left to chance... especially on this mission.

Bronk and Party would both have the explosive code for the vehicle they would share. They would be in the most dangerous and up close exposure, as they would be responsible for getting Allie-Mo in position for his part of the play. If one of them were to be captured or killed the other would be responsible for blowing up the car. If they both were incapacitated, Brandy had a trigger which would take care of business.

Butter was the *gatekeeper* and *preventer* for all information which would place members of the team where they needed to be at the correct time. The *gatekeeper* was responsible for relaying electronic and visual data supplied by the many cameras he had overridden with programs which would obliterate surveillance tape of his team. Every door, window, passageway and camera in The Drake Hotel was in Butter and Sherm's computers. Should either be incapacitated, the other would carry on with the mission. Butter would be in an office building two blocks from The Drake appearing to be just another working stiff, putting in extra hours all the while guiding Andy, Party and Allie-Mo through the maze of security which surrounded the President.

Each move had to be choreographed to the split second in order to get close enough for the termination. He would prevent any incidental threat or person from sneaking up behind his team. He guarded the 'back door' via cameras and constant monitoring of all security communications.

The *'site'* was somewhere between the underground parking garage and the grand banquet hall on the fifth floor where the President would attend a $20,000.00 per seat fund raiser. Working people all over America were losing their jobs as a result of the financial policies of this 'share the wealth" President. His administration and others, who ostensibly supported the policy by paying $20,000 to get a seat at the party, seemed not to be bothered by the dichotomy. It was quite the accepted, blind mantra of the times in the United States of America.

The prime target area was somewhere between the elevator and the sixty yard long grand foyer and entrance to the expansive room which would contain the event. Sixty yards was precious little distance in which Allie-Mo could accomplish his task.

The mass of security personnel, photographers and news media would create a chaotic inter-mix of human debris and equipment which had to be negotiated by Party, Bronk and Allie-Mo. Getting close enough for the termination was almost totally dependent on the crowd flow and luck. As well planned as the operation would be, *luck* was the one thousand pound elephant in the room. There was little chance that Party, Bronk and Allie-Mo would not be stationed within the sixty yards, but luck would play the major part in accomplishing the mission.

The plan called for them to be positioned near the elevator door and then work their way along and among the throng of news people who were on hand to record the fund raiser event for posterity. Party and Bronk would literally have their hands on Allie-Mo's back, guiding and pushing him toward his target. Once close to the President, the rest was up to Allie-Mo. There was no doubt that he would pull the trigger if he got close enough, but it was up to Party and Bronk to signal the abort if it appeared that the mission could not be fulfilled.

Everything had to happen in a split second, because this individual, filled with hate, could not be compromised if it was not possible to bring the mission to fruition. Party would hold Allie-Mo by the belt and would stop all forward progress if, in his determination, the situation would not allow for a positive conclusion.

The unknown factor would be Allie-Mo himself. He had been drilled over and over that if not this time, there would be another time and that if he was given the signal to abort, that he would abort and not shoot from a distance that possibly would not kill the President. Would his heightened state of emotion of being this close to the man he so hated, succumb to the control of Party and Bronk, or would he explode into a rage which would sabotage the mission? Party and Bronk were totally reliant on the training and brainwashing which had been administered to Allie-Mo over the past three months. It was a blatant draw to an inside straight and they knew it. If the termination was successful, Party and Bronk would have to slide back through the chaos that was sure to follow, and descend five floors before disappearing into the crowd of protestors and supporters in the street. Allie-Mo was dispensable and left to the secret service or preferably to the coroner.

CHAPTER 17

After putting on the clear latex gloves, a part of the uniform over the next couple of days, everyone departed the Citation and headed toward the terminal. Three vehicles were positioned at the curb as the team exited the terminal door. The three drivers who had delivered and were standing by the cars, left their post and walked south under the canopy which covered the sidewalk. After they had walked about fifty yards, a black Suburban wheeled out of the line of traffic, pulled to the curb and the three drivers entered the passenger side doors and the Suburban pulled back into the traffic flow and disappeared into the night.

Party, Bronk and Allie-Mo took the first car, a 1989 Buick LaSaber. They loaded their small overnight luggage into the trunk. Party slid in behind the steering wheel, Allie-Mo was shotgun and Bronk sat behind him in the back seat. Party guided the Buick into the incessant traffic flow.

Sherm threw his bag into the back seat of the 1996 Camry, assumed the position under the steering wheel and cut sharply into traffic at his first opportunity.

Brandy opened the driver's door and in one smooth motion threw his luggage into the front seat and seated himself in the 1999 Sebring. He quickly entered the torrent of traffic and headed for the exit at Central and 63rd Street.

While each team member had assigned duties and designated positions in which to carry out the mission, they were really on their own for the next forty-eight hours. Everyone had a safe house or apartment for sleeping, eating and relaxing. There would be very little contact between the team until three hours before the attempt.

Chapter 17

The plan was in place and now only time remained as the temperate of patience.

CHAPTER 18

Party guided the Buick into the single-car garage of a house on Archer Avenue, a couple of blocks from US Cellular Field. He, Allie-Mo and Bronk took their bags from the trunk and entered the clean well-kept home. There wasn't much furniture, just the essentials; a breakfast table, four chairs, a living room couch and two cheap wingback chairs. The three bedrooms each had a double bed and a dresser with a table lamp at one end.

Party lead the way down the hall, threw his bag into the first bedroom on the left, motioned Bronk toward the room on the right and escorted Allie-Mo into the room on the back corner of the house. He then flipped on the light in the small bathroom as he entered to take a piss.

Bronk went to the kitchen and removed a bottle of water from the refrigerator and opened a package of beef jerky. There were six vacuum packed packages containing plastic forks, spoons and knives lying on the countertop next to the coffee maker. The pantry contained twelve REM's, along with bread, crackers, peanut butter, jelly, catsup and four cans of sardines. Party always had to have his sardines, no matter what the mission or where he was. Bronk had tried eating the little fish, but he had not developed a taste for them.

"Well, it's not a palace, but it will keep the rain off our head," Party said as he entered the kitchen. "I'm a bit hungry. Ya'll want something to eat?" he asked as he took one of the cans of sardines to the sink. The kitchen air immediately assumed the fishy smell of the sardines as Party pulled the ring and peeled the lid off the can.

Chapter 18

"Mmmmm, come to daddy my little tasties," Party said as the last drops of the oily liquid drained from the can. He popped a paper towel off the roll, laid it on the counter and sat the can on top of it. Next came the catsup and crackers. Party was deep into enjoying his favorite snack.

CHAPTER 19

Andy bent over, enduring the pain which had acquired momentum in his lower back and removed the door chock he had put in place before he went to bed. Even though he had slept in many more uncomfortable and hostile situations, the mattress on his temporary bed had not been kind to him. Deep furrows appeared on his forehead as he looked into the mirror attached to the back of the door.

"God, I hope this doesn't have anything to do with age," he mused as he smoothed his rumpled hair.

He had heard rain hitting the roof during the night and with little light entering the room around the window shade, he assumed that Chicago's gloomy weather forecast was in fact true.

Opening his door, he checked the bathroom to see if either Party or Allie-Mo were using the facilities. The bathroom door was open, so he grabbed his kit and crossed the hall. He could swear that there was a lingering, fishy smell hanging in the air. Party had already been in the bathroom. He flipped on the fart fan and reached to turn on the shower. Again, the stiffness and mild pain in his back.... Nope, it had nothing to do with age.

As Andy closed the bathroom door, he could hear Party in the kitchen singing.... "I Can't Get No Satisfaction." It was rather painful to the ear since Party could never carry a tune in a bucket, but Party did love his 60's music and had forever sang when he was pre-occupied with un-important activities.

The water was hot and stung his back as he tried to get the spray to relieve the nagging soreness in his body. Turning and twisting slightly seemed to help accomplish the feelings of yesteryear. After his shower and drying off with the large grey towel, Andy pulled on his jeans and blue and gold shirt and walked barefoot into the hall toward the living room and the kitchen. The wood floors creaked and were cold under his feet.

Allie-Mo was sitting on a kitchen chair in front of the picture window. He sat rigidly on the chair staring into the morning fog and rain. He did not appear to notice anything that was happening around him. Andy had been trained to always be aware of his surroundings. Not being aware could have gotten him killed many times over.

Party was seated at the kitchen table, a hot cup of coffee in front of him and a rather day-dreaming look on his face. Andy had never seen such a placid look on the leader of 12 Squared.

"You make me wonder what in the world you are thinking," Andy said with a testy edge to his voice.

"Oh, nothing really, I'm just lining up my intended schedule for occupying that cabin on the lake. I have an option on a small home on a beautiful lake not far inland from the coastline in North Carolina. I'm ready, Andy... I'm ready. After this mission, my time has come."

"I think it's time for all of us, Party. After all that we have been through over these years, we still have some time to experience what people call a normal life," Andy said as he made his way to the coffee pot. He patted Party on the shoulder as if to re-enforce his belief that there was still time.

"I will tell you, my friend, that my few brief months in Georgia, have given me a taste of what is possible on the flip side of our lives to this point. I really like my home, the yard work, the daily chores, drinks on the front porch swing and the normality of what I know my life can be," Andy said as he leaned against the kitchen cabinets and sipped his hot coffee.

"You know Andy, we have lived a thousand lives compared to most people. We have been both fortunate and deprived of what people call normal lives. We are fortunate that we have been a part of so many history making events, yet deprived and unfortunate in the family and every-day life aspects of the masses. It is what it has become.

Andy pulled a chair away from the table and shot a glance at Allie-Mo, still transfixed at the living room window. As he sat down, Andy wondered what was going on inside Allie's head. After all these years, he could not recall ever really being afraid that he might be experiencing his last hours on earth as he prepared for a mission. The thought was not in his head now. He wondered if Allie-Mo was having thought of possibly his last few hours.

Party got up from his chair, poured another cup of coffee and opened the refrigerator for a piece of fruit. He picked up, and seemed to study closely, the MRE package which would pass as breakfast on this rainy, bleak day in Chicago.

Allie-Mo sat at the living room window until eleven o'clock. He took note of Party and Bronk by issuing a brief nod accompanied by, "Good morning, sirs. There is much rain today." He picked up an MRE and took a bottle of water out of the refrigerator. Returning to the living room, he squatted in the corner next to the front door, opened the packet and quietly consumed the contents.

Chapter 19

Party and Bronk looked at each other and understood the mutual concerns they had. Was this young Arab man, so filled with hate, capable of following his training once in place and only steps away from the person to whom he directed his intense hatred; The President of The United States?

At 12:30 PM the black two-way radio toned and a familiar voice said, "The landscaping is complete .... The trees are ready for delivery."

Things were in place. All of the electronic surveillance and articles of fulfillment for the mission were where they needed to be and operational. The 'tree', Allie-Mo was ready for delivery to the target area.

The rest of the day and early evening for Party and Bronk was spent reading, listening to the news on television, watching people and cars on the street and bidding good-bye to the clouds and rain as the weather front moved south and east. By nine o'clock, the skies were clear and a cool crisp breeze made the huge, lighted American flag over the stadium, move in a graceful, rippled rhythm. If the mission is successful, that flag would soon be flying at half-staff and a nation's society would be on trial.

The night time hours were always the worst for Andy. The limited vision and the shadows of possible peril had many times disguised the potential dangers associated with the mission. He had always trusted his team, but the nagging possibilities of what might interfere with the task at hand, was a constant with him.

Party had seemed to never give thought to anything but the meticulously planned steps toward accomplishment of the mission. Nothing had ever back-fired on them to the point that the plan had to be severely altered. Party planned every aspect

Chapter 19

of the missions and his track record was impeccable. The Brigade was bulletproof with Party's planning.

The night was quiet and Andy slept peacefully. Reviewing and rehearsing the mission was left for tomorrow.

Chapter 20

"Cool, crisp morning," Party said as he greeted Andy in the kitchen. "Supposed to be a rainy and wind event moving in this afternoon ... good for planting trees. Any rain gear can become confusing for security," Party said as he gazed out the kitchen window.

Andy poured himself a cup of coffee and turned to inspect the once again rigid figure at the living room window. Allie-Mo once more seemed in a complete meditative state of consciousness. He sat with stiff posture and eyes transfixed on the existence of the world outside.

Party would talk privately with Allie-Mo in the late morning and then about 3:00 PM. He would instill in Allie-Mo's thought process the planning and purpose of the mission, the instructions for every step of getting into the hotel, the process by which the final approach would be carried out in synchronized timing and above all the absolute necessity to abort the mission should circumstances merit. Allie-Mo had to thoroughly understand that success was dependent upon the plan and that if not tonight, there would be another time and place.

The essential outcome of the mission plan was to assassinate The President of The United States. There could be no partial fulfillment of the mission. It was all or nothing.

After going over the plans and checking with the 'landscape crew' in a brief twelve second communication over the walkie-talkie radio, Party looked at his latex encased hands, gave Andy two-thumbs up and turned to look at Allie-Mo. The conversation that was about to take place would result in the final appraisal of Allie-Mo's mental preparedness of what the plan required of him. Party would do the talking. Andy would sit quietly and conduct an evaluation of Allie-Mo's physical reactions as Party focused and re-focused the step-by-step plan. Andy closely studied Allie-Mo's body language as Party engaged the mission's wild card. Eye movement and pupil dilation were critical in the mental state of the young Arab who would take the life of a human being he hated so much.

Allie-Mo showed no outward irritation at Party's re-grinding of all of the details and timing of the mission. He sat peacefully, answering Party's questions and verifying that he understood every step of the final seconds preceding the shots he would fire.

The most important part of the entire mission was that Allie-Mo would absolutely comply with the abort signal if given by Party. Allie-Mo said he understood and would do as Party instructed. Andy was convinced that Allie-

Mo's mental state was right on and that he would act only as prescribed by the plan.

Party took one final look into Allie-Mo's eyes gave him a slow, controlled high-five and while standing up, grabbed his chair and returned it to the kitchen.

There was no plan given to Allie-Mo for after he had fired the shots. Party had not advanced any hint of what would happen when the target had been eliminated. Allie-Mo had never asked for a plan. Party and Andy took it in stride that Allie-Mo understood that whether captured or killed, it was a dead end destination. Allie-Mo did not care what might happen to Party and Andy, and by intent, there was a reciprocal agreement about Allie-Mo. Death was the accepted possible consequence. It was something with which 12 Squared had always known. Evidently Allie-Mo did also.

Chapter 20

After a lunch of MRE's, chicken and rice and a dry biscuit, all three men spent time rehearsing the walk-thru movements which would place them next to the President. After walking through the planned movements five times and critiquing each rehearsal. Party opened the closet just inside the front door and removed a medium sized canvas bag. He placed the bag on the couch and un-zipped the large zipper which allowed the sides of the bag to fall away, exposing a somewhat standard looking camera carried by all 'on the scene' cameramen covering news events.

The camera was fully functional for filming, but it had modifications which made it a killing machine. Mounted atop the camera, just behind the lens was a five-inch tube about one-inch in diameter. The front of the tube housed a high intensity LED assembly. When switched on, the light illuminated a six-foot by six-foot area. Even the most dimly lighted area and subject to be filmed was clearly visible. On the surface, the tube appeared to be like most other modern camera lights.

There were a couple of 'latest technology designs in firearms' which made this camera light very unique. Inside the tube were five .45 caliber exploding cartridges positioned heel to toe. The assembly was a ceramic devise designed and manufactured by a small off-the-grid group located somewhere in the Texas panhandle. The design contained no moving parts... no trigger, no firing pin, no hammer and was basically invisible to electronic scanning. The actual bullet was a polymer compound encapsulated within thin ceramic jackets, which was designed to exit the tube and explode once initial penetration had affected the target.

The rounds would be triggered by an electronic impulse from a small battery and not by a firing pin striking the jacket. The ingenious design resulted in one of the most lethal, two-second, throw-away weapon in the world. There was no long-range killing with this. It was designed for one reason ... to positively kill something in an up close and personal manner.

Party placed the camera on Allie-Mo's shoulder and made some adjustments to the foam-rubber pad which cushioned the contact with the camera. He then walked through the rehearsal several times until each man understood and felt comfortable with the maneuvers which would get them in place for accomplishing the mission.

Once they were in place in the media camera line in the great hall, the firing mechanism would be activated on the camera. All Party, Andy and Allie-Mo could do then was wait for their opportunity.

CHAPTER 21

The first round would hit the President in his left hip which would cause his leg to buckle and then he would fall forward toward the line of cameramen. Four more rounds would be fired in split second succession starting at just above the waist, striking the torso and ultimately the President's head.

The entire sequence would at first appear as though the President had stumbled as he walked. Not until the third round would blood be readily visible as the waist and lower torso rounds exploded after finding their target. It would all be over in an instant. Then, the ensuing screams and chaos would send everyone scurrying for cover. All in attendance would instantly know that something was terribly wrong. Over the wild screams would come... "the President is down"... "the President is down!"

Secret Service would swarm to cover the President while several agents would draw their weapons and search for the source of the non-discernible assault. They would look left and right, up and down, all the while moving to try and assess the situation and surrounding. People would be screaming and scrambling for refuge. Tuxedos and evening gowns would create a mass of movement on the floor, along the walls and toward any exit. Party and Andy would be engulfed in the torrid flow of bodies. Allie-Mo was on his own.

Cameramen would at first fall back, but true to their nature and learned culture, they would re-group their cameras and their positions and once again continue to record all they could as witness to the event which would stun the world. The Kennedy tapes would have nothing on what they were recording for posterity. Through all of the pushing and shoving, cameras would gyrate wildly. Pictures of the floor, ceiling, people's asses and backs, people's feet and blurred shot of the great hall would find themselves in the recorded history of clips when the President of The United States was assassinated.

Party and Andy would crawl quickly to the fire escape stair door before the Secret Service could scramble to secure it. Andy would quickly shut the door behind them and place a small wooden wedge under the door which would delay others from using the door just long enough for the decent of two flights of stairs. Once on the second landing, they would open the cold air return vent which had been equipped with a concealed swing away hinge just two days before. They would enter the three foot by three foot sheet metal duct, reach above their heads, grasp a loop in the rope taped to the corner of the duct, close the return air vent and then silently lower themselves three floors to a remote area of the main lobby.

If all went well, the cold air return on the backside of the elevator shaft would not have security personnel around it and Andy and Party would exit the duct grill. No security camera covered the area behind the elevator shaft. While Andy closed the grill, Party would reach behind a large insulated pipe and push a small garage-type devise anchored inside the insulation wrap. The devise triggered a release of the rope anchored in the duct system. The rope would fall into the plenum return in the basement. If ever discovered, the rope would be considered as some type of rigging left by maintenance workers.

If all went well... That was the unknown reality.

CHAPTER 22

The queue for credentials check for the media personnel was set up at the east entrance to the hotel. Reporters and their camera crews waited impatiently to go through security, so they could then start to set up their cameras and lighting bars. Most of the cameramen had been witness to many such political bull-shit gatherings over the years with many administrations. This was just another assignment which might keep them from night-time happenings, held out as possibly being a lot more exciting and adventurous. Anyhow, they were here trying to make the most of it. Cell phones, iPads and idle conversation filled the time.

It was imperative that Party, Andy and Allie-Mo appear as calloused and bored as they could when their press passes and credential were checked. They, in no way, could give away that they were replacements for three hopelessly drunk and drugged Channel 23 employees sleeping it off in the back of the company van. They would awaken to find out they had missed their assignment, which would mean they probably would have some explaining to do to their boss and producer.... But, then again, maybe their camera malfunctioned and they just didn't get the 'tape at eleven' footage.

CHAPTER 23

The apparently new junior officer checking badges seemed thorough in his approach and scrutiny of the plastic clad credentials of everyone in line. Andy knew they were fortunate to not have an officer who had years of familiarity with reporters and cameramen. This was their first stroke of luck.

After looking at the picture on the lanyard-held credentials, studying closely the face which appeared thereon, the new officer nodded and waved the crew past the screening post. Party, Andy and Allie-Mo were no exception. As their badges were being checked, two female officers were checking out the camera, cell phones, pens, pencils, and notebooks. After inspection, the equipment was un-ceremonially pushed to the end of the table. They gathered their gear and proceeded into the service entrance of the hotel. They moved nonchalantly among the other press people and ascended the guarded staircase to the fifth floor ballroom area.

Here, they moved more swiftly to establish the position the wanted and had to hassle with another cameraman for their spot. Allie-Mo became irritated with the guy but reached a staring contest agreement as to who had what territory. Party took a firm grip on Allie's arm and told him to relax. There was an ever so slight look of tension in Allie's eyes, but he nodded his head and complied with Party's instruction.

After a few minutes, all of the press people were ready to get on with the task of covering the story. White House staff continued to move up and down the intended entry path the President would take. Press summary and talking points were passed out by the staff as the routine ground toward what was expected to be an evening filled with glitz and glamour. Political figures and the *'would-be-nears'* began to parade toward the ballroom. Senators, Representatives and their wives, powerful business people, celebrities and a various array of people who could afford the high-priced ticket to the event, strode down the aisle, smiled and posed for the cameras, and blissfully marched toward their assigned tables. Party and Andy played the part of still-life, portrait cameramen by pressing the flash button on cameras which had no picture card.

Andy looked at Allie-Mo several times and was relieved to see the calm which engulfed his body and face. Allie was in the zone he needed to be in. He was ready and from time to time pretended to be filming the passing array of people before him.

Party checked his watch. Even though he knew there was bound to be a delay in the arrival of the President, he moved to Allie's left side and readied to give him the hand signal to carry out the mission.

There should have been that stillness and almost surreal aura in the moment which was always there in the minute or two before the commission of the final task of the mission, but everything was crystal clear. That bothered Party for just an instant, but his vision, albeit in slow motion, moved approximately twenty-five yards to the right as flashes of light and a sudden excitement penetrated the air. The President and First Lady, smiling and waving in front of their entourage were making their way down the broad isle and stepping confidently toward history.

Step by step, step by step, the entire sequence moved slowly toward Party, Bronk and Allie-Mo. Party and Allie-Mo knelt down, one knee on the floor. Party put his right hand inside Allie-Mo's belt and pants. His left hand was on Allie's upper left arm. Party started the step count. Beginning with the left foot... seven, right foot... six, left foot... five, right foot... four, left foot... three, right foot... two....

Andy simultaneously released Allie's left arm and jerked his hand out of Allie's belt band.

As the President's left foot came forward, the first round struck its mark into the left hip. The President's leg gave way; he stumbled and started to fall forward. The remaining four rounds, within one and one half seconds, found their mark. The last round entered his head just above his left eye. Each round exploded within a mil-a-second after impact.

The first Lady had recoiled in surprise as the President appeared to stumble and as the first round struck. She remained out of the line of fire. She screamed as blood splattered the President's white shirt.

The chaos began. Screams, yelling from the Secret Service... "the President is down"... "the President is down"... People in the entourage were running into each other and screaming as they tried to escape the hysteria which gripped the room. Hardly anyone dropped to the floor as instructed by the Secret Service. Everyone, who was in close proximity to the President and First Lady, made a mad rush away from the scene. Party had planned and expected the reaction and he and Andy used the stampeding bodies to shield their movement toward the fire escape door. There would be no alarm or video on the door. Butter had made sure of that with his computer from blocks away.

Andy and Party stayed as low to the floor as two sixty something guys could get and became part of the mad rush toward the main staircase. Both men got to the steel door and quickly slipped into the stairwell. Andy placed the wooden block under the door and followed Party down two flights of stairs. They opened the cold air return grill and slid into the duct, closing the grill behind them. Just as the grill closed, they could hear the stairwell fire door slam against the wall and within seconds people were descending the stairs and passing by where Party and Andy were concealed in the duct.

Andy reached up and grabbed the loop on the rope in the corner of the duct, secured his grip and slid silently down and away from Party. As Andy descended, the next loop on the rope appeared and Party grasped it, stepped off the small flange which secured one piece of duct to the next and also disappeared into the darkness.

It was a quick descent down three floors. Andy waited for Party to arrive next to him. They both looked through the louvered grill to assess the area. Seeing no one, they pushed open the hinged louver and crawled into the back lobby. Party reached behind the insulated pipe, found the small device and pushed the button. The rope could be heard slithering its way down the duct toward the return plenum in the basement.

Although they knew that the hotel's video cameras had been disabled, Party and Andy pulled their baseball caps close to their eyes and quickly blended with the mass evacuation which was pouring out of the hotel. As they cleared the front doors, they removed their press credentials cards and the lanyard and stuffed them in the front pocket of their jeans. The continuous pressure from behind then pushed them quickly into the street where traffic was stalled due to the number of people coursing between cars.

Chapter 23

Andy glanced at his watch... 7:43. By now, Butter had left the building where he had been positioned and would be proceeding to a bar eight blocks away. The chilly evening air had lured many local apartment residents, carrying their umbrellas in case of rain, to the sidewalks. Andy and Party walked at a casual but steady pace among those either heading home or destined for a night out for drinks and eats. After the first block, there seemed to be no awareness of what was happening at the hotel. They covered the nine blocks to Mahoney's Bar in about twelve minutes. Mahoney's old neon sign welcomed them inside.

The plan, including a beer at Mahoney's was on track. The volume on the televisions was being turned up as live coverage of the swirling chaos in front of the Ambassador was being depicted on the screens. Many people were calling for quiet so as to hear what the news person was reporting. The frantic reporter tried to relay information about the 'attempted assassination of the President' at the hotel. That story line would hold for a while as government officials rounded up the Vice President and the Speaker of the House to take control of the government. Now, the bar was absolutely silent except for the blaring televisions. Everyone but Andy and Party was in total disbelief.

"So much for getting that beer," Party whispered to Andy.

The coverage on the television was an array of benign footage of the President's entry into the grand foyer to the moment of the first indication of something gone terribly wrong. Then the cameras depicted the floor, ceiling, butts, back of heads and chandeliers. Rapid movement of the cameras was a clear indication of the confusion and scrambling of the cameramen. The scene was one of complete pandemonium. It was impossible to identify Allie-Mo within all of the chaos for the five minutes of the television coverage. And then, as a stable camera panned the scene, there was Allie-Mo, with his camera still on his shoulder, kneeling and filming the President's body from about ten feet away.

When the Secret Service realized his presence, Allie was thrown to the floor and held down by three agents. His camera had hit the floor, lens first and had broken into several pieces. Agents grabbed Allie under his arms and dragged him further away toward the ballroom. Allie-Mo had not tried to run. He had stayed to savor his victory.

Butter had been experiencing the deadly quiet and utter disbelief at Duffy's. Only the television's blare broke the silence. He stepped over to the wall at his right to watch the screen. Right at this moment, he was a long way from Andersonville.

Andy checked his watch. Sherm would pick him and Party up in eight minutes across the street from Mahoney's. Brandy would pick Butter up at Duffy's. The Buick that Andy and Party had used had gone up in flames beside an old abandoned warehouse near Cottage Grove Avenue and 87th Street as they walked to Mahoney's. Butter's car was burning near Lakeview and Clark Street and Sherm's Sebring would meet the same demise at Route 64 and Gary Road. All four men would then be transported via a plumbing repair truck to Du Page Airport. A flight plan had been filed nine hours previously for a private jet going to Terra Haute, Indiana. *Maintenance issues* would ground the plane there for almost two days. Party would lay low and observe what transpired from his motel room and transact business with a buyer from Columbia for the plane.

CHAPTER 24

The flight to Indiana was extremely quiet. Other than the faint engine noise and the clink of ice cubes in empty glasses of Jack Daniels, everything was very somber. Each man seemed deep in his own personal reflections of the past few days and of the life they had led for so many years.

From Viet Nam, Panama, Nicaragua, Czechoslovakia, Germany, Iran, Iraq, Egypt, Pakistan, Afghanistan and other 12 Squared engagements around the world, there sprung many memories and bonds which held these warriors together. Soon, it would be all over, but the memories would live with each man until his death.

After deplaning, men known as Bronk, Party, Brandy, Sherm and Butter exchanged solid handshakes and robust bear hugs. Party reached into his leather backpack and pulled out a bottle of cognac.

"We should be drinking Gentleman Jack or Single Barrel, I guess, and God knows we have a special attachment to our favorite brother Jack Daniels, but I elected to depart on this one hundred and thirty year cognac. Hope you don't mind." Party handed the bottle to Sherm and reached again into his backpack. He produced six small, antiques liquor glasses, giving one to each of his trusted brothers-in-arms. Party removed the wax from the top of the bottle, removed the cork and placed the bottle near his nose. He inhaled deeply.

"Yes sir, I think this will be appropriate for the occasion." Party carefully poured the aged cognac into one of the glasses and set it on the ground in the circle formed by the remaining brigade. That one represents all who served with us over these many years. He next poured into the glass of each man, poured his own and raised his glass. I salute and drink to The Twelve Squared.... All who were and the five of us, who in a few moments, will be no more. "Here's to The Twelve Squared."

Andy looked into the eyes looking back at him and knew that he would never again see any of the individuals who had been a part of his life for thirty-five years. Now, everyone knew the ride was over. Their final act had become reality and the time had come to bring the proverbial curtain down.

"Short-n-sweet," Butter said as he and Andy shook hands. "But like the raven... Nevermore," Butter said as he gripped Andy's hand. "Nevermore."

Andy already knew that he was never going to see Butter again. Even though Andy planned to stay in Andersonville for at least a short while, he knew that Butter would not be serving him the 'coldest beer in the south'.

"Parting is such sweet sorrow, my friend," Party said as he and Andy looked at each other with curiously sad and knowing eyes. "The adventure started just yesterday, progressed through a millennium of time, and has come to an end here. The mission has been successfully fulfilled. After all, it's nothing personal... Right?" Party squeezed Andy's hand and then pulled him close to his chest.

"Can't let this swill go to waste," Party said as he took a defining slug of what remained of the liquor in the dark brown glass bottle, passed it to Andy, turned and walked toward the hanger.

Andy, after turning the bottle up, swallowing the warm cognac and passing the bottle to Sherm, saluted his

Chapter 24

comrades and walked toward the terminal.

The bottle was passed from Sherm, to Brandy and finally to Butter and after drinking, each took their leave to who knew where.

The small glass of cognac remained on the tarmac.

CHAPTER 25

Present Day

"Shut off your recorder, now."

"So, there you have your story, Mr. Brueman. What I have related to you over the past two days is what led up to the successful assassination of a President of the United States," Andy said as he carefully evaluated the face of someone who had just been told the story of the murder which rocked the world.

A pale and haggard journalist sat silently for several moments.

"Do I believe what you have told me is your hidden question within that comment," Jack Brueman mused as he peered over his half glasses and into the eyes of a man whom he understood only had days to live.

"As un-believable as your account of the assassination may appear to be, ... Yes, I believe you. What really gets me is the fact that so little, other than the fact that the assassination did take place and that an Arab man was captured, confessed, tried and found guilty of the assassination, is known about the background leading up to the moment of the attack. Your story fills in a lot of unanswered blanks on many many pages concerning the assassination. For years, literally thousands of investigators and their best efforts have not been successful in finding out how and why this came about."

"But, yes, I believe you."

"Might have been another story if Allie Mo had lived," Andy said as he further chided the veteran journalist who had been around long enough to have pretty much seen and heard it all.

Chapter 25

"He became a martyr for his family and his religion when he grabbed that court officer's gun and initiated the shootout. Allie was an expert handling weapons and if one really looks at the video tape of what unfolded in the courtroom, those who know about such things, know Allie committed suicide that day. Due to the high tension of the moment and the over exuberance of the court officers, Allie-Mo was killed. He did not shoot one officer and no one in the room was hit. You may want to review that tape, Mr. Brueman."

"Allie-Allesia Mohammad had his day in court, told his story, and got his revenge and his seventy-four virgins. He had been prepared to die for his cause at any time after he was recruited to kill the President. It's almost impossible to stop someone with that fundamental mindset. Actually, I hope he has been fucking his brains out."

"I find your story so compelling that it is difficult, at the moment, to even ask you questions. I'm used to digging, badgering and in some cases, shamelessly pursuing what facts or secrets have not been told. Crap, with you, Andy, there seems to be nothing to go after. You have not let me 'do my job'."

"On another level, let's say that this story you have told me is true, what do you expect to be the end result of bringing all of this to light now?"

"The truth is something which is hard to discern these days. Truth is many times trumped by the ability of the damn political benders to bring information to their advantage. They give a shit about anything other than what will benefit them. So many of your brother journalists, during that administration of their intended messiah, did not do anything but bring harm to America. You were some years younger when all of that went down... you could not have been more than a struggling reporter with no influence... just building your resume."

"I'll tell you one thing; all of the journalistic whores of those days were traitors. Just because the bastard had dark skin, you, as a group, were dishonest with yourselves and with citizens and downright traitors to America. At least some of the most realistic among you have finally admitted they were wrong. Lot of good it does now."

Jack Brueman took the verbal lashes and placed his hands on his knees.

"I can't argue with your analysis, Andy. The press fucked up and committed a real disservice to America. Even though only a few admit it today, I think we all knew. Clearing many of the left-winged, numb-nuts, dumb asses out of the journalism cesspool has not been easy. History and time combine to make a very lethal cycle for the grim reaper."

"Is there another, deep-seated, particular reason you are now telling me this story?"

"I'm telling you this story now, so that history can be set straight and not be the enigma of thousands of brains questioning or supposing why the assassination took place. That damn Kennedy thing will go on forever. There was a myriad of reasons behind our actions twelve years ago, but the overriding one was that we had to rid our country of the worst son-of-a-bitch to ever sit in the oval office. He was destructive to our country and he had to go," Andy stated rather matter-of-factly.

Andy paused and stared out the window into the garden.

Chapter 25

"Everyone is gone now. At least I believe they are. Within eight hours of the assassination, we were all off the grid, under anyone's radar and such. Not like any of us really ever existed in all reality, but we simply disappeared. Our years of secret operation were known by so very few, our daily existence and personal lives were covered completely with false identities, so, we, therefore never really existed as part of this world."

"Butter is the only one I'm not sure about. He was younger than all of us. To this day, I have not heard of him showing his face at Butter & Dave's. All of us older guys have passed or in my case are passing through. In a short while, the undertaker will not really know who he is putting in the ground. Pretty amazing, don't you think," Andy questioned as he again returned his eyes to a rather dismayed journalist who would dateline the block-buster story of recent times.

"Questions... Comments, my young journalist friend?" Andy mockingly asked as he felt the automatic dose of morphine concoction surge through the vein in his left arm.

Jack Brueman assumed a rigid posture in his chair and nodded his head.

"I understand the motive for the assassination as you explained it. The years of programs, put into law while he was President, have proven to be detrimental to our nation. And, believe me, coming from a very liberal family life and educational background, if I had not opened my eyes and mind to the reality of the world, I would still have my head up my ass and among the believers behind big government. Disastrous people can bring about disastrous results."

"But ..."

Chapter 25

"It remains difficult for me to fully comprehend what your team did and then just vanished from the face of the earth... yet, here you are... right before my eyes. You ask me if I thought the whole story and this band of existent/non-existent brothers of yours is amazing. It's more than amazing. The whole story you have related to me is beyond everyday comprehension. It's a fucking movie script... that's what it is, and I know you have told me the truth. Yes, Mr. Bronk, I believe and don't really have any further questions."

Andy fell silent for several moments before he returned is eyes to Jack Brueman's expression of ... *what's next?*

"I'm going to make you famous, Jack."

"Can you handle it, Mr. Brueman? A lot of people will brand you some god-damned kook, you know."

There will be no collaboration of what you print. Nothing can substantiate all of your literary prowess. Why will anyone believe you... after all, your source will be dead... and who was he anyway? Maybe he was just an old man who made up a good story and convinced you, young pup, that the story is real. Safe houses... where were they in the millions of houses in Chicago. Exploded, burned out automobiles will be commonplace in the annals of police and fire department records of routine calls. What is your proof, Mr. Brueman?"

"Think about how you will handle being called a fucking kook. It will affect your life for as long as you live. Probably the only or at least the main by-line on your epitaph will key on the fact that you were the guy who revealed how and why a President of The United States was killed. Think about it, my friend."

Chapter 25

Andy paused for several moments as he studied the contemplative face before him.

"I ask you to think on it and decide quickly, because I only have a short time in which to tell this story to another journalist," Andy said as he smiled and patted Jack Brueman's hand.

"Tell me, my friend, are you ready to fill in the blanks of history and become famous?" I must know before you walk out of this room. My story is done with you."

"God-damn it, Andy. You have appealed to my journalistic ambitions and yet strung me up by my balls and threatened to cut them off!" What in the hell have you done to me?"

Jack Brueman paused and studied the crystal blue eyes staring back at him.

"You know I want it, so, yes I will publish your story."

Jack Brueman felt the weight of the world hit him and almost instantaneously lift him off his feet and vault him toward outer space.

"Yes sir, I will publish your story. Can I withstand the critique of what I publish will be told by the passing of time. Hell, it's like putting in golf and pussy... *'Never up, never in'*. After all, what can anyone do to me, I'm just the frigging messenger!"

CHAPTER 26

After sharing part of the Jack Daniels, from the small silver flask he carried in his right side coat pocket, Jack Brueman shook Andy's hand and left the treatment center. He knew there was no chance that he would ever see Andy again. The ball was in the air now. All that was needed was for the journalist of the hour to hammer it to the court on the other side of the net. Jack Brueman was on his path of destiny.

While there was no strong, single theme in his mind, a million sub-sets of formats and headlines were exploding in the deep recesses of his brain. He didn't need to rush to meet a deadline. He was the deadline.

He drove slowly through the almost deserted streets back toward the interstate. His mind was exhilarated but his body ached as though he had been going through his long abandoned workout routine at the gym. The derelict muscles of his body screamed for relief from the pain.

The particularly painful areas were the back of his legs and his gluts situated in the less than supportive driver's seat of his now ten year old Buick.

"I guess you were sitting and listening with a puckered ass, Jack," he said to himself as he entered the freeway and fell in behind a flatbed hauling two large CAT earthmovers.

"You may need one of those in a short while, son," Jack blurted out to the windshield.

The response of the old Buick was sluggish as he again slammed the accelerator to the floor in a painfully slow attempt to pass the flatbed. As he neared the Kenworth's driver's door, the hauler's name, Junior Cummings, USA Haulers, Inc. was visible in bold letters. Junior was from Athens, Georgia.

"Hey, Junior... I bet you wish you knew what I know," Jack Brueman sang out in an almost child-like rhyme. He didn't know why he taunted Junior with his knowledge, but the relief of telling someone seemed beneficial toward relieving his soul of the burden which he had accepted. He wanted to take the next exit and go back and tell Andy that he had changed his mind... that he couldn't accept the responsibility which Andy had handed him. He wanted to take the exit, but glanced only briefly at the inclined road as he floored the accelerator of the Buick and assumed the identity of an Indy 500 driver racing toward victory and hell.

The Beginning

Coming soon, the next book in this series to be released 2015.

If you have enjoyed this book, please leave a review for the author on Amazon. Thank you

About the Author

Richard W. Hobson was born February 7, 1945 in Knoxville, TN.

America was in the midst of war and difficult times accentuated the mood of the country. His father soon departed the scene and raising a new baby became the responsibility of his mother.

After a third marriage, his mother settled down to a life in Cape Girardeau, MO. "Bill" was in the fifth grade and exhibited interest in art and writing about things he saw daily in his life. High school literature and English classes inspired his interest in writing closing songs for student talent shows and entering poems for high school anthology competitions. A poem, "New Born Calf" was his first successful entry.

He self published his first poetry book, "Days To Days", while living in St. Louis.

Subsequent moves up the corporate ladder and relocations to Flint, MI., Toledo, OH, and finally to Phoenix, AZ., filled his life with human experience which contributed to his understanding of people's emotions, human strengths, and frailties. He continues to write about many of the personalities he has encountered during his life.

"A Single Candle" was the poem which inspired him to gather many of his poems and publish "Us Until Now". Bill has never received a rejection notice, only encouragement from his family, friends and even strangers who have read his poems and other works.

Look for his other two books "The 365 Club" and the poetry book "Us Until Now"